Rita
the Rescuer

Rita
the Rescuer

Hilda Offen

Happy Cat Books

For Katie and Helen

HAPPY CAT BOOKS

Published by Happy Cat Books
An imprint of Catnip Publishing Ltd
Islington Business Centre
3-5 Islington High Street
London N1 9LQ, UK

This edition first published 2002
3 5 7 9 10 8 6 4

A CIP catalogue record for this book is available from the British Library

ISBN 10: 1 903285 41 0
ISBN 13: 978 1 903285 41 1

Printed in China for Compass Press Ltd

There are four children in the Potter family
– Eddie, Julie, Jim and Rita.

Because Rita is the youngest, the others
sometimes leave her out of their games.
They say they have to spend all their time
rescuing Rita – she falls in the mud, she
gets stuck up trees and she loses her
wellingtons. Poor Rita!

"Take me with you!" begged Rita
one day.

"You're too young!" said Eddie. "You
can't push or pull."

"You're <u>too</u> young!" said Julie. "You can't skip or jump."

"You're too young!" said Jim. "You can't run or kick."

Eddie, Julie and Jim went off to play with
their friends. Rita was left alone with the
cat.

"You'd like some milk, wouldn't you?"
said Rita and she went to get it in from the
doorstep.

"What's this?" she cried. "A parcel – for
me?"

Rescuer's Outfit said the label inside.

First Rita unpacked some boots, then gloves and tights, a tunic, a belt and a cloak.

"Oh!" she said. "That's just what I need."

And she put them all on as fast as she could.

9

In the street some children were jumping over a rope.

"Let me try!" said Rita.

"You're too young!" they said and they held the rope even higher.

But Rita wasn't put off.
She drew a deep breath, gave
a hop, step and jump and –
up she soared!

Rita could hardly believe
what was happening.
"Look at me! Look at me!"
she shouted.

Rita's leap carried her high above the roof-tops. She could see for miles. Down in the next street she spotted Basher Briggs who was snatching her brother Jim's football.

"GIVE THAT FOOTBALL BACK!"

Rita's roar was so loud that all the windows round about rattled.

Basher turned pale.

"I'm off!" he said and he dropped the football and ran away as fast as he could.

"Thanks a lot," said Jim.

"You're welcome!" said Rita. "Now for my next rescue!"

She could hear someone close by yelling, "Help! Help!"

A pram had rolled into the river. Worse
still, there was a baby inside! The current
was sweeping it away and no one could
reach it.

Quick as a flash, Rita dived into the water. She grasped the pram firmly and swam to the river bank.

The ducks quacked and the people cheered.

The mother hugged her baby and shook Rita's hand.

"You deserve a medal!" she said.

Rita was about to reply when she heard a scream. There, on the other side of the river, was her sister Julie. She was being chased by a bull!

In a split second, Rita was there.

She flung herself in front of the bull, who stopped dead in his tracks.

"Bull – you're a bully!" said Rita.

She stared straight into his little red eyes, while Julie escaped over a gate.

The bull looked ashamed and shuffled his hooves; but Rita was already on her way.

It was Lavinia Smith's wedding day.
There she was, with her flowers and her
bridesmaids – but the car had a flat tyre.
Mrs Smith looked furious and Mr Smith
was in a panic.

"Oh no, the foot pump doesn't work!" he
cried.

Rita came bounding over a hedge.

"Leave this to me, Mr Smith," she said.
"It won't take a minute."

She gave a mighty puff.

"There you are. That's fixed it!" she
said.

"Thank goodness for the Rescuer!" cried
Lavinia as the car roared away down the
street.

Nearby in Jubilee Gardens a large crowd had gathered beneath a tree.

"That cat's going to fall!" someone yelled.

"Our poor little Rufus!" cried Mr and Mrs Rumbold.

"Hang on, Rufus!" called Rita. "Here I come!"

She whooshed through the air like a whirlwind.

"Ooh!" gasped the crowd.

"Got you!" said Rita and she snatched Rufus to safety just as his claws slipped from the branch.

"Thank you! Thank you!" cried Mr and Mrs Rumbold, but Rita was off again – she had heard another call for help.

Eddie's go-cart was out of control and hurtling down the steepest hill in town.

Rita ran like a greyhound.

She grabbed the go-cart and braked so
hard with her heels that sparks flew in the
air.

"Phew!" said Eddie, as they screeched to
a halt. "That was a very close thing!"

At the foot of the hill a crowd stood and
stared.

Mr Carter's mare, Rosie, had fallen down
a hole in the road. No one knew how to get
her out.

But help was at hand.

Speeding down the street came
– a jet plane?
– a javelin?
– a flash of greased lightning?
No! It was Rita the Rescuer.

Rita dived down into the hole.

"One – two – three – heave!" she cried.

She raised Rosie above her head.

"Up you go!" she said and she lifted
Rosie out of the hole and placed her
back safely on the road.

"What strength!" cried the crowd.
"What muscles! Did you ever see anything
like it?"

They cheered and they clapped and Rosie
swished her tail.

"Goodbye, everybody!" said Rita.
"I'm off home for my tea!"

But she stopped on the way to hit two thousand runs –

to kick four hundred goals –

28

and to skip up to three thousand and
eighty.

"What a busy day!" said Rita, back
home in her room. She took off the
Rescuer's outfit and hid it under her bed.

"Everyone's talking about the Rescuer!"
said Eddie at tea-time. "She's terrific! Who
can she be?"

"Where can she come from?" asked Julie.

"However does she do those rescues?"
cried Jim.

Rita could have told them, but her secret
was special. So she smiled to herself, picked
up her spoon, and started eating her beans.